MONSTER
and Boy

Henry Holt and Company, *Publishers since 1866*
Henry Holt® is a registered trademark of Macmillan Publishing Group, LLC
120 Broadway, New York, NY 10271 • mackids.com

Library of Congress Control Number: 2019949519

ISBN 978-1-250-21783-7

Our books may be purchased in bulk for promotional, educational, or
business use. Please contact your local bookseller or the Macmillan
Corporate and Premium Sales Department at (800) 221-7945 ext. 5442 or
by email at MacmillanSpecialMarkets@macmillan.com.

First edition, 2020 / Designed by Mallory Grigg

Printed in the United States of America by LSC Communications,
Crawfordsville, Indiana

10 9 8 7 6 5 4 3 2 1

For Susan Bloom,
who believed in all of us.
—H. B.

For Danny,
my partner in crime
25/07/2020
—A.S.

MONSTER
and Boy

Hannah Barnaby

Illustrated by Anoosha Syed

GODWIN BOOKS

Henry Holt and Company
New York

monster

boy

1.

Once there was a monster who loved a boy.

The monster had never met the boy because monsters are nocturnal and boys (well, most boys) are not. But he knew the sound of the boy's voice, and he loved that sound. He knew the smell of the boy's dirty socks, and he loved that smell. He knew the sight of the boy's slippers by the side of the bed, waiting for the boy's feet, and he loved those slippers and those feet.

Monsters don't know much about love.

Or maybe they do.

The monster had lived under the boy's bed for many years. He listened to the boy playing during the day. He

listened to the boy talking in his sleep
at night. He heard bedtime stories and
songs, he heard snoring and snuffling,
and he loved the boy more and more.

One night, the boy's mother read
him a book. A book about monsters.

"I'm not afraid of monsters," he
heard the boy say.

"Of course not," said his mother.
"There's no such thing as monsters."

I'll show her, the monster thought. And as soon as she closed the door behind her, the monster pulled himself out from under the bed. He stretched. He stood. And he looked at the boy.

crack!

"Hello," the monster said.

The boy was silent. The monster thought maybe the boy couldn't see him, so he made himself light up.

"Ta-da!" the monster said.

The boy took a deep breath and opened his mouth, and the monster knew he was going to scream.

The monster panicked. He did the only thing he could think of.

He swallowed the boy.

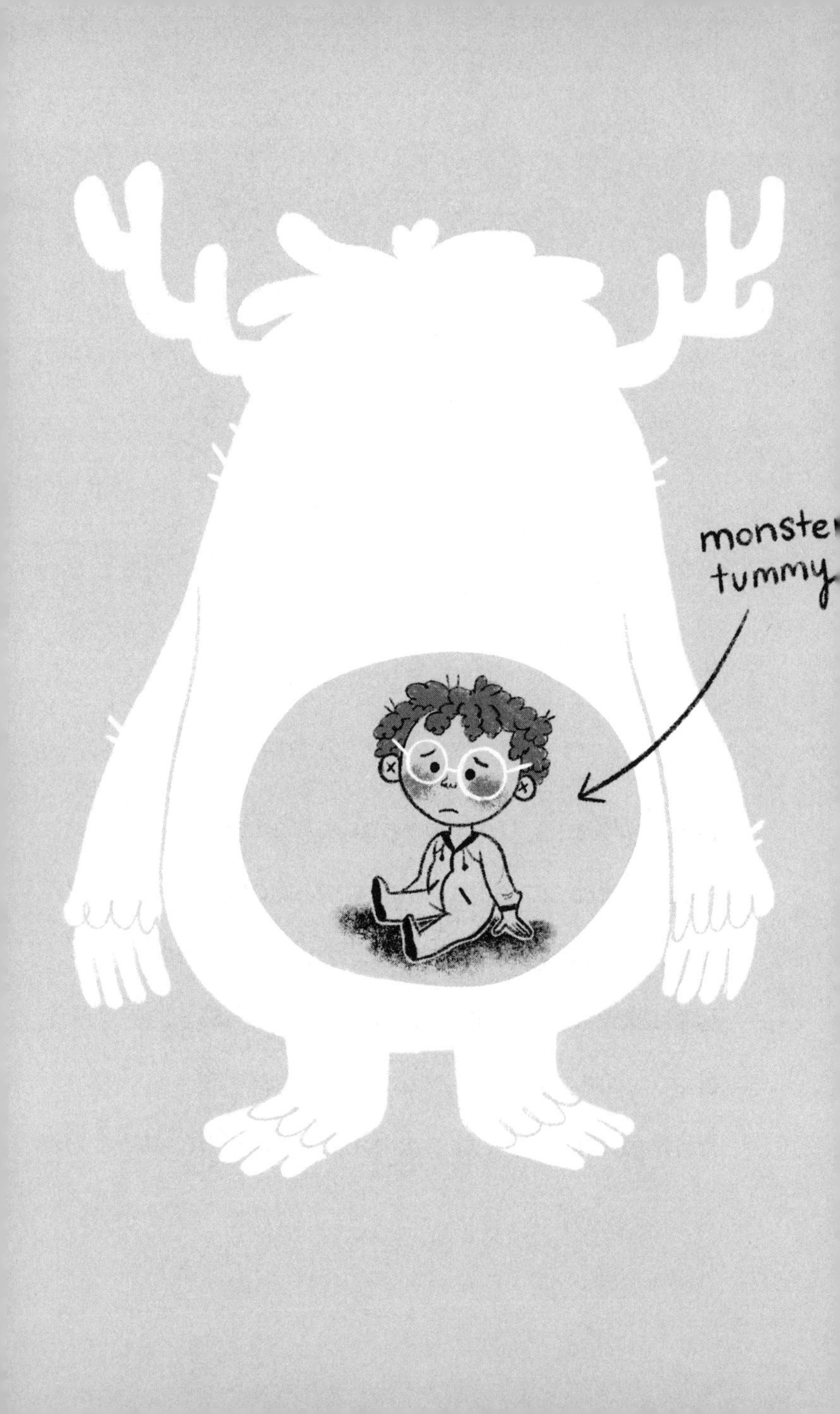
monste
tummy

2.

This story is not quite what you were expecting, is it? When a story begins with the word *Once*, it seems like you know what you're getting into. The word *once* is tricky that way, because it means that whatever happens in this story happened only *one time*, and therefore it could not possibly happen to you, too. But *once* also means that every story is different. Anything is possible.

If it makes you feel any better, I am also quite surprised by what just happened. In fact, I have no idea what's going to happen next.

Does that make you feel better?

No?

We'd better keep going, then.

3.

The monster was instantly sorry that he'd swallowed the boy. The boy felt strange in his stomach, heavy and nervous. The monster did not like how it felt, and also he missed the boy terribly.

Then he heard a small voice from inside himself.

It was not his conscience. It was not his soul.

It was the boy.

"I'd like to come out, please," said the boy.

"I'd like that, too," the monster replied.

"Then let me out," said the boy.

The monster put his hands gently on his belly. "I don't know how."

His belly was silent. Then the boy said, "My mother says there's no such thing as monsters."

"Hm," said the monster. "I think she's wrong about that."

"I'm starting to think so, too," the boy told him. "Maybe she forgot about monsters when she grew up."

The monster thought about this. It made sense to him, but it also made him unbearably sad because the boy would grow up, too, and then the monster wouldn't be believed in anymore.

The boy yawned. It was warm inside the monster, and dark, and he was getting sleepy. The monster swayed gently back and forth until the boy fell asleep. He snored a little, and it tickled the monster's stomach in a pleasant way.

The monster was a bit less sad now, but he was still lonely. And he still didn't know what to do.

THINK, he told himself, but as soon as he did, his mind went completely blank.

Isn't that always what happens?

Soupbone

Bobert

+

ted

Mozart

+

BRANCH

jimminy

and sal

4.

georgi

+

peppe

stevie & cog

McKenzie

Here I shall tell you that even though the

monster and the boy had not properly

introduced themselves to each other,

they both had names.

However, neither the monster

nor the boy has properly introduced

himself to *me*, either, and so I

SAM

AND TOOT

KEVIN

Jack & Jill

don't know what their names are.

Do you?

Ah, well. Let's make some up. We'll call the monster Reginald, and we'll call the boy Grover.

No?

Soupbone and Ted?

No.

Big Magic and Earl?

No.

Well, why don't you go ahead and make up your *own* names for the monster and the boy, and I'll just keep calling them the monster and the boy. There's only one monster and one boy in this story, so it won't be too confusing.

At least, I don't think so . . .

Li'l Stinker

Big Magic Earl

Reginald and Grover

butter fingers

MAXIMUS and MAX

eddy

Pickle + Skipper

5.

The monster sat there, with the boy he loved sleeping in his belly, and waited for his mind to fill up again. Then he thought.

buuurp!

He thought about making himself burp. He thought about tickling himself until he laughed so hard that the boy came flying out of his mouth. He thought about calling his mother and asking for advice.

But burping was embarrassing, and he didn't want the boy to hear him do it. And tickling yourself is very nearly impossible. (It is. Try it. Go ahead, I'll wait for you.)

And although his mother was
nocturnal, too, she didn't like talking
on the phone.

won't
pick
up

Then a very particular, rather naughty thought scrolled slowly through the monster's head.

He had gotten used to the feeling of the boy in his belly.

He almost liked him there.

If he kept the boy, he wouldn't
have to miss the boy when he left
for school in the morning, because
the boy wouldn't go to school at all
anymore. And wouldn't that make
the boy happy? Wasn't the boy always
complaining about having to get up so
early and get dressed and eat breakfast
and get on the bus?

Now he wouldn't have to do *any*
of those things! The boy would be so
happy!

The monster couldn't wait to tell
the boy the good news.

But the boy was still snoring away,
and the monster was tired from so
much thinking and so many feelings

and all that swaying. He needed some rest.

The monster crawled under the boy's bed and, thinking happily of what he'd say to the boy when they both woke up, he fell asleep.

He woke up some hours later, as the moonlight crawled across the floor and crept its bright fingers under the edge of the monster's home. He came out, blinked, stretched, and then he noticed something. Something terrible.

His belly felt light and empty.

The boy was gone.

Thump!

6.

The monster felt all around his belly. He jumped up and down. He wiggled back and forth. But he didn't feel anything. He was empty.

"Oh no!" he cried. And then he really cried. He cried so hard that he gasped for air and then began to cough.

He coughed again and again and again, and then once more. He coughed so hard that something flew out of his mouth.

It was about the size of a grasshopper. But it wasn't a grasshopper. It was the boy.

"What happened to me?" he squeaked.

"You . . . got tiny," the monster said.

"Does this happen to everything you swallow?" the boy asked.

The monster shrugged. "I don't know. I've never swallowed anything before."

"Never?" the boy asked.

The monster shook his head. "I've always just been under your bed."

The boy was amazed. "You've never had cookies? Or pizza? Or broccoli?"

"No," the monster said sadly.

"That's a shame," said the boy. Then he got a strange look on his face.

Alarmed, the monster asked, "What's wrong?"

The boy looked up. A tiny, tiny tear rolled down his tiny cheek. "Talking about food has made me really hungry. And I don't know if I'll ever get to eat those things again, either. Maybe I'll have to live under the bed with you."

This thought delighted the monster for exactly four seconds, and then it didn't.

"Do not worry," the monster told the boy. "We will fix this."

"How?" asked the boy.

"I do not know," admitted the
monster.

He looked around the boy's room.

There were many, many things in the
room, but he didn't know how any of
them worked or what they were named.

"Do you have anything that makes things bigger?" he asked the boy.

"I have a magnifying glass," said the boy. "It makes things *look* bigger."

The monster considered this. "That may not be enough. But it's a start."

The boy was much too small to get the magnifying glass, and he couldn't remember which drawer he had put it in, so the monster had to look for it. Since the monster had never seen a magnifying glass, he spent a rather long time pulling things out of drawers, holding them up, and asking, "Is this it?"

And each time, the boy said, "Nope."

Finally the boy suggested that maybe he should describe the magnifying glass. "It's round," he said, "with a straight handle."

The monster found a round thing with a handle.

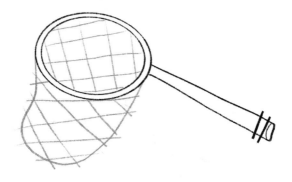

"No," said the boy, "that's a net. A magnifying glass has a part you look through."

"Like this?" asked the monster.

"No," said the boy, "that's a kaleidoscope. That won't make me look bigger. It will just make it look like there are a lot of me and we're all mixed up."

The monster quickly dropped the kaleidoscope. "No, thank you!" he exclaimed. "We have quite enough trouble already. What else does the magnifying glass look like?"

"It's silver," the boy said.

"Round and silver and you can look

through it . . . got it!" The monster held up the magnifying glass.

"Almost," said the boy. "Those are handcuffs."

"Drat it all!" shouted the monster, and he slapped at the drawer in frustration. The drawer flew out of the dresser and fell onto the floor with a tremendous noise.

(Have you ever noticed how much louder noises are when you are trying very hard to be quiet? Even little noises and medium noises and especially embarrassing ones? Well, this noise was like the loudest, most heart-stopping trying-to-be-quiet noise you have ever heard.)

The monster gasped. The boy
clapped his hands over his mouth, even
though he hadn't said anything.

They both waited for someone to
come running into the room.

But no one did.

And there, on the floor—right in the middle of everything else that had fallen out of the drawer—was the magnifying glass.

7.

"You found it!" the boy told the monster.

The monster picked up the magnifying glass and held it to his eye. He looked at the boy. "You do look bigger!"

he said. Then he put the magnifying glass down. "But now you look smaller again."

"That's to be expected," said the boy.

"Is there any way to use this . . . differently?" the monster asked.

"You mean, to make things *get* bigger instead of *look* bigger?"

"Yes, I guess that's what I mean."

The boy squinched his eyes. He held his tiny hand to his tiny chin. He pulled his tiny mouth to one side. He looked like he was thinking very, very hard.

He thought for so long that the monster started to feel hope swelling up in his heart like a big balloon. Then the boy said,

"No, I don't think there is."

The monster's heart balloon deflated. "Nothing?" he asked. "What about using *two* magnifying glasses? Or saying some special words while I look through it?"

"Like *abracadabra* or *presto*?" suggested the boy.

"Yes!" said the monster. "What kind of words are those?"

"They're magician words," the boy told him.

The monster chuckled. "Silly," he said. "There's no such thing as magicians."

The boy started to say something, but a strange noise interrupted him. The monster gasped.

The boy put his tiny hands on his tiny stomach. "I'm really hungry," he said.

"Don't you have anything to eat up here?" the monster asked.

"I'm not allowed to have food in my room," the boy told him.

Rumble Rumble

The monster didn't know very much about food or eating, but even he could see that a net or a kaleidoscope or handcuffs or a magnifying glass was not going to make the boy bigger for good. He could also see that they were not going to make good snacks.

The monster sighed. He held out his hand. "Climb on," he told the boy.

The boy nestled himself into the monster's palm. "Where are we going?" he asked.

The monster took a deep breath. "Downstairs," he said.

8.

Here I shall tell you something else: The monster was very, very afraid of downstairs. Most monsters are. This is because monsters almost never leave the bedrooms where they live, and their own mothers have warned them about the dangers of doing so. Monster mothers are quite different from human mothers, and they tell their little monsters all kinds of extremely frightening stories about places they've never seen before.

Why do they do this?

Does it make the little monsters grow up into big monsters who are good at telling scary stories?

Or do the monster mothers remember how they were frightened by their own mothers?

Sometimes people—I mean, monsters—just can't be bothered to figure out a different way to do things.

But now, this monster was about to do something very different indeed. He was going to take the boy downstairs, even though he had no idea what awaited them. He was going to do this because he loved the boy, and the boy was hungry, and downstairs was where food lived.

Also because deep down, underneath where he felt afraid and nervous and a tiny bit ill, the monster felt something else. He didn't know what it was called, but I do.

It was curiosity.

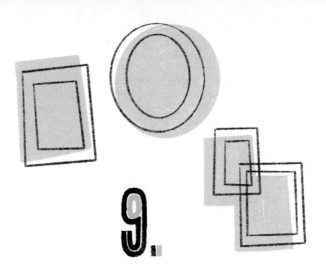

9.

The monster stood at the top of the stairs. He sneaked his toes out over the edge and then scooted them back. He did this three times before he had the courage to put his foot all the way over and down onto the first step. He wobbled a little.

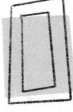

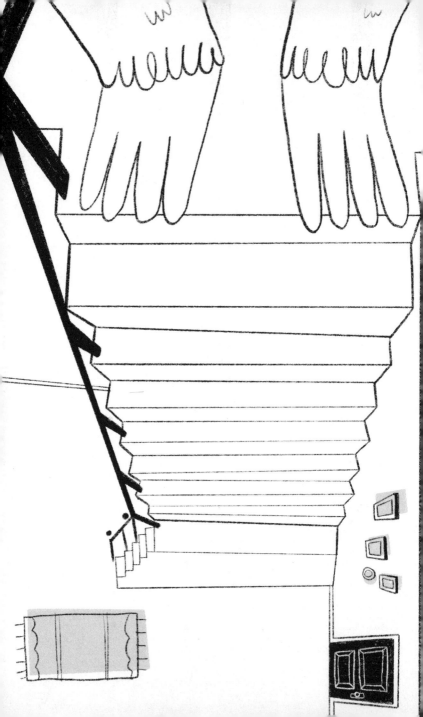

"Hold the railing," the boy told him.

"What's a railing?" the monster asked.

"The bar right there." The boy pointed.

The railing was smooth and shiny and went straight as an arrow along the stairs. The monster looked at the stairs, which went out and down and out and down like a zigzag. They made him dizzy. He looked at the railing again.

"Sometimes it's called a banister," the boy offered. The monster liked that word very much. It sounded a little bit like *monster*. He decided something. He curled his hand around the railing.

"Hey!" cried the boy as he and the monster slid all the way down the banister and landed neatly at the bottom of the stairs.

"It's a good thing your voice got
tiny along with the rest of you," the
monster told him. He said it as quietly
as he could without whispering. He
did not want to whisper, because
when monsters whisper, it is often
mistaken for growling. (Dogs have the

same problem. I'm sure you know that already.)

But even though the monster spoke quietly, it was—perhaps—not quite quietly enough. Because before he and the boy could move, there was a noise. It came from the kitchen. And then a voice said, "Who's there?"

The monster felt a feeling in his stomach, as if the boy was still in there.

He almost wished the boy *was* still in there.

"Oh no," whispered the boy. "It's my mother!"

10.

The monster and the boy were very, very
tempted to run right back up the
stairs and hide under the bed where
they belonged. Well, the monster was
tempted. But then he remembered that
the boy didn't really belong under the
bed. He also remembered wanting to

prove to the boy's mother that she was wrong about his not existing.

Although he hadn't planned to do that by shrinking her son. And he was pretty sure she'd be mad about that. And *that* made him want to run up the stairs all over again.

But the monster loved the boy. And the boy was hungry. So the monster took a deep breath, puffed out his furry chest, and pretended he was feeling brave.

(Sometimes that's all it takes to get your feet to move forward.)

The monster peeked through the doorway into the kitchen.

Every cabinet was open. Every
drawer was open. The refrigerator, the
oven, and the dishwasher were open.

And someone was running around the kitchen looking into every open thing. But it was not the boy's mother.

It was another monster.

The boy gasped. The kitchen monster froze. The under-the-bed monster said, "What are you doing?"

The kitchen monster slowly turned

around. Her eyes were wide. She was small for a monster, barely tall enough to reach the upper cabinets. "I heard a loud noise." Then she whispered, "I'm looking for candy."

"Monsters don't eat candy," said the under-the-bed monster.

"That's not a monster," the boy told him. "That's my little sister."

"But she looks like a monster," said the monster.

The boy rolled his eyes. "That's a suit. Trust me. She's just a little sister."

She looked at them both. "I think I might be the *big* sister now."

"That's not how it works," the boy replied.

"What happened to you?" she asked.

"It's a long story," he said.

"It's all my fault," the monster told her. "I swallowed him. I made him small."

The sister-monster looked at the under-the-bed monster and said, "That was not a long story at all." Then she laughed.

"I'm not sure I like your sister," the monster told the boy.

"Sometimes I'm not sure I like her, either," the boy said.

"I don't care if you like me or not," the sister-monster said to the monster. "But you're taller than I am, so if you help me find the candy, I'll help you fix what you did."

"Don't help her," said the boy.

"Okay," said the monster.

"If you don't help me, I'll wake up Mom and Dad," said the sister-monster.

"Um . . ." said the monster.

"I can count backward from a hundred with my eyes closed," said the boy. The monster thought this was a very poor time to bring this up.

"So can I," announced the sister-monster.

"I don't believe you," said the boy.

She squeezed her eyes shut. "One hundred, ninety-nine, ninety-eight . . ."

The boy whispered to the monster, "We can talk in there," and pointed to a doorway.

The monster carried the boy
through the doorway and into a room.
The room was small and had three
shiny white things in it. Two of the
shiny white things were not full of
water. One of them was.

"What *is* this place?"

"It's a bathroom. We use it for . . . Oh, I don't have time to explain. And it's kind of gross, anyway."

It's a little-known fact that monsters are terribly afraid of water. The monster tried very hard not to look at the shiny white thing that was full of water, but he could feel it looking at him.

"So, we need to figure out a way to—" the boy started, but suddenly the shiny white thing full of water made a noise, and the monster jumped.

When he jumped, his hands jerked. Both of them.

Especially the one upon which the boy was standing.

Because the boy was so small, he
didn't weigh very much.

Because he didn't weigh very much,
he flew into the air.

Because he did not have wings and
could not continue flying, he came

down again and landed in one of the shiny white things.

And because this was quite possibly the worst day of both the boy's life and the monster's, the shiny white thing the boy landed in . . .

. . . was the one full of water.

11.

There was a tiny splash.

The monster made a noise that is difficult to describe, but if I had to spell it, it would look like this: "WAAAAOOONOO."

(Maybe there should be a few *F*s and *P*s and *H*s in there, too. Spelling noises is rather difficult. If you haven't tried it before, you should. But not right now. This simply isn't the right time.)

"What was that?" the sister-monster called from the kitchen.

"I don't want to tell you," the monster called back. He was sure that if she found out what he'd done, she would wake up her parents. He tried to remember how he had made himself brave enough to come downstairs, but he couldn't, and anyway that wasn't enough bravery to stick his hand into a big bowl full of water.

He did manage to gather just enough bravery to peek into the water, and what he saw astonished him.

The boy was floating. No, he was more than floating. He was . . .

"What are you doing?" the monster whispered.

"I'm swimming!" the boy told him. "In a toilet!"

The monster was very relieved. "Good for you!" he said. "Now climb out."

"It's too slippery," the boy said. "You need to pull me out."

"Oh no," said the monster.

"What's going on in there?" called the sister-monster.

"Nothing!" the monster assured her.

"Help!" yelled the boy.

"No, thank you!" yelled the monster.

But the sister-monster was already

standing there. "If you two don't want

Mom and Dad to wake up, you really should—what are you doing in the toilet?"

"Swimming," the monster said helpfully.

"Gross," said the sister-monster. Then she looked at the monster and put her hands on her furry hips. "Do you need my help?"

"Yes!" called the boy. His voice echoed off the sides of the toilet bowl, so he really called, "Yes-yes-yes-yes-yes!"

The monster sighed. "Yes," he said in a very small voice.

"I will help you," said the sister-monster. "If you help me find the candy."

"I can see it from here," the monster told her. "It's on top of the shiny box."

"Can you reach it?" she asked.

"Definitely," he said.

"Okay," she said, and she left. Then she came back.

She was holding a small green net.

"Not the fishnet!" the boy cried.

The sister-monster rolled her eyes. (Her real ones. Not the ones on her costume.) "Hold still," she told him. Then she scooped him into the net and dropped him into another shiny white thing. One that wasn't full of water.

The boy shivered. The monster held out his hand, and the boy looked at it for a moment before climbing on.

"Here," said the sister-monster, and she handed the monster a washcloth.

"Thank you," said the monster.

"I think that's for me," the boy told him. "To dry off."

The sister-monster grinned. "Now," she said. "CANDY."

She led them back into the kitchen.

"This is a bad idea," said the boy, wrapping himself in the washcloth. "Mom doesn't like it when we eat candy after bedtime. And the wrappers make a lot of noise."

"Hm," the monster said. "I can fix that." He carefully set the boy down on the kitchen table and reached for the bowl of candy. Then he rolled himself into a ball around the bag so his fur muffled the sound of the unwrapping. When he stood up, all the unwrapped candy was in his hands.

candy wrappers

"Wow," said the sister-monster.

The monster handed her the candy. She stuffed it all in her mouth at once.

"Now tell me how to make your brother big again," the monster said.

She shrugged. "Mmalssvtbls," she mumbled.

"What?" the monster and the boy said together.

The sister-monster swallowed hard. She bounced up and down on the balls of her feet. "Mom always says vegetables make you grow. But I think she's wrong. I think we grow when we're sleeping. So you need to go to sleep, and then you'll get bigger."

"That's a terrible idea," the boy said. "What if I wake up and I'm not any bigger and I've wasted the whole night sleeping?"

The sister-monster shrugged again. "Maybe you're just small now."

The monster and the boy did not like this idea, either. But as soon as she said it, they looked at each other and each of them saw the same sadness in the other one's eyes.

"She may be right," the monster said.

"I hate it when she's right," the boy said.

"I'm always right," said the sister-monster. "I'm going back to bed now." And she went upstairs, hopping and wriggling all the way, leaving her brother and his monster standing in a kitchen where everything was open and all hope—and candy—was gone.

12.

Here I shall tell you that while it is **not** true that little sisters are always right, it *is* true that mothers are. And when the sister-monster said *go to sleep*, it reminded the monster of something that his own mother had told him about monsters. (Monster mothers *mostly* tell scary stories, but they do tell some nice ones, too.) He hadn't believed her, of course—he had thought it was just a silly story she had made up to get him to go to bed when she wanted him to— but now he had a funny feeling in his belly that was a little bit like the feeling of having swallowed a boy he loved, but different.

This is what the monster mother said:

Monsters have a special way of
making dreams come true.
Anything a monster dreams is what
the world must do.
When you sleep, what's all around
turns into what you see.

So close your eyes, and make the
world a bit more monsterly.

Isn't that sweet?

Well, actually, maybe it's a little
strange. Because it means that
everything we think is real is here only
because a monster dreamed it. And if
a different monster dreams about it
a different way, it could change. Your
school could turn into an amusement
park. Your dog could turn into a
velociraptor. Your mom could turn into
a robot and your dad could turn into
a cardigan sweater and your car could
turn into a hot dog . . . and you . . .
and I . . .

Oh, dear. Now I've frightened myself.

I'm going to snuggle with my teddy bear.

Do you think I can still trust him?

Back to the story.

13.

"Did I dream you?" the monster asked the boy.

"What?" the boy asked.

"Never mind," said the monster. He didn't actually want to know the answer, because he loved the boy so much that he thought it might break his heart a little to find out. But he did have a whole new idea of how to fix him.

"I have bad news," the monster said.

"Oh no," the boy said nervously.

"Your little sister was right. Well, almost. One of us does need to go to sleep. But it's not you. It's me."

"This doesn't seem like a very good time to take a nap," said the boy.

"Oh, but it is," the monster told him. "And while I'm sleeping, you need to whisper in my ear."

"What do I need to say?" the boy asked.

"You need to tell me a story," the monster said, "so that the story becomes my dream, and my dream can make you big again."

"Okay," said the boy. "But before we go back upstairs, did you want to try a cookie?"

The monster shook his furry head. "Definitely not," he said. "I'm not taking any more chances with swallowing things."

"Well then," said the boy, "can you at least get *me* a cookie?"

"Of course," the monster told him. So he did, and then he carefully closed each and every cabinet that the sister-monster had left open.

(Not all monsters are so inconsiderate, you know.)

Then he took the boy back upstairs to his room, and all the way up, the monster held the banister with one hand while the boy sat nestled in the other, happily eating a cookie the size of a sled.

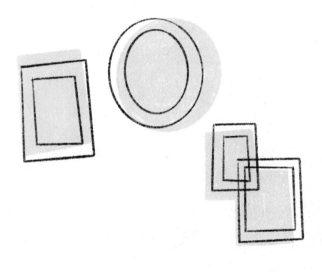

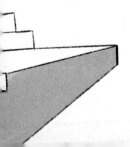

When they got back into the boy's room, the monster set him gently on the floor and tucked himself under the bed. "I'm going to sleep now," he told the boy. "Don't forget about the story."

"I won't," said the boy.

The monster was quite sure that his plan would work, but he was also a little bit afraid that it wouldn't. He knew that the boy's mother read him stories every night. Surely the boy could tell this story in the right way and then everything would be all right.

But stories have a way of getting carried away, don't they?

Sometimes unexpected things happen.

The monster felt tears pricking at the corners of his eyes. "Most stories have happy endings, don't they?" he asked the boy.

The boy nodded. "Oh yes," he said. "Most stories have endings that are just right. And if the ending isn't right, it's probably not the end."

The monster sighed happily. "I'm sorry I swallowed you," he said.

The boy smiled and rested his hand on the monster's nose. "I'm not," he told him quietly. "That was the best cookie I ever had."

The monster yawned. "And I'm sorry I dropped you in the toilet."

The boy patted the monster's nose gently. "Yeah, that part was pretty gross."

The monster sighed. "I love you," he said. And then—hopefully, bravely—he closed his eyes.

And the boy began the story.

"Once there was a monster who loved a boy . . ."

the end

14.

You didn't think that was really the end, did you?

I have so much more to tell you, and besides, it's bad luck to end a story on an odd-numbered chapter. My granny taught me that, and Granny Waffleton was never wrong about anything to do with stories. (Bears were another matter altogether.)

Anyway, I am happy to report the following things:

1. The boy's mother had just cleaned that toilet, so it wasn't really *too* disgusting that the boy went swimming in it.

2. The boy's mother had also figured out that the sister-monster was hunting for candy at night, so she very cleverly put a bowl of candy that was made from sugared beets and sweet potatoes on top of the refrigerator, and therefore what the sister-monster actually ate was a whole bunch of vegetables.

3. The monster's plan worked like a dream (ha-ha, get it?), and when the boy woke up the next morning, he was his regular size again.
He was still a bit damp from his unexpected swim, but all things considered, that wasn't so bad.

But of course, when the boy woke up, he also knew for certain that his mother had been wrong. Monsters were real. And the feeling of knowing that was a little bit like the feeling the monster had while the boy was in his belly. It can be lovely to have a secret, all heavy and low in your tummy, but it can also be slightly uncomfortable.

And that feeling got more uncomfortable than lovely at bedtime the next night, when the boy's mother read their usual story about monsters.

After she kissed the boy and quietly closed his door, he whispered, "Are you there?"

"Yes," whispered the monster.

"Do you want to come out?" asked the boy.

"Okay," said the monster.

The boy lay very still while the monster crept out from under his bed. He didn't want to startle the monster and get swallowed again.

The two of them looked at each other.

Neither one of them moved.

Then, very slowly, the boy's mouth curled into a smile.

And the monster's did, too.

Then the boy began to giggle.

And the monster did, too.

"Remember when you knocked the drawer down and everything fell all over the floor?" the boy said.

"Yeah," said the monster.

"Remember when I thought your sister was a monster, too?"

The boy laughed harder. "Remember when I went swimming in the toilet?"

The two of them laughed harder and harder until they almost couldn't breathe. Then they sighed at exactly the same time.

The boy rubbed his eyes. "I'm glad you're real," he told the monster.

"I'm glad you're real, too," said the monster.

The boy dug his fingers into the monster's fur. The monster patted the boy's hair.

And they fell asleep that way, both of them holding the secret of each other deep down inside.

the end

seri

i mean it.

Hannah Barnaby has worked as a children's book editor, a bookseller, and a teacher of writing for children and young adults. Her first novel, *Wonder Show*, was a William C. Morris finalist. Hannah lives in Charlottesville, Virginia, with her family.

hannahbarnaby.com

Anoosha Syed is a Pakistani Canadian illustrator based in Toronto. She has a passion for creating cute, charming characters with an emphasis on diversity and inclusion, and has illustrated many best-loved picture books.

anooshasyed.com